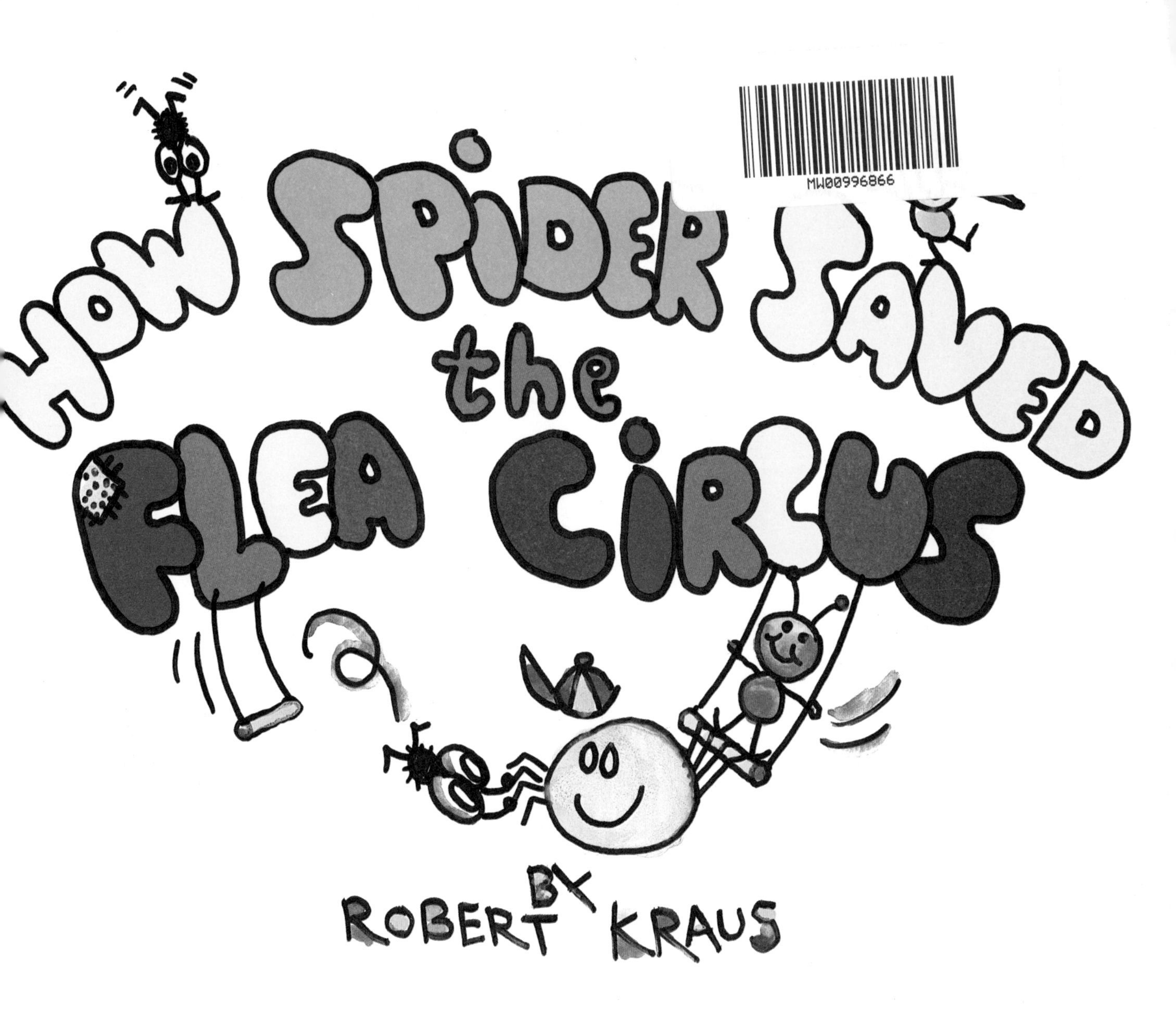

SCHOLASTIC INC.
New York Toronto London Auckland Sydney

ISBN 0-590-42459-9

12 11 10 9 8 7 6 5 4 3 2 1 2 3 4 5 6/9

Printed in the U.S.A. 24

First Scholastic printing, September 1991

I was walking down the street whistling a happy tune. I was going to meet my friends Ladybug and Fly.

They were looking at a big poster on the wall.
The flea circus was coming to town!
"What fun!" said Ladybug. "I *love* the circus more than anything!"
"And it's the Bugley Brothers circus—they're the best!" said Fly. "Let's go and see it!"

BUGLEY BROS
FLEA CIRCUS
THRILLS
A FLEABAG SHOW
CHILLS
ONE DAY ONLY

"May I come, too?" I asked.
"Well, I don't know," said Fly.
"Of course you may," said Ladybug. "Three's company."

"I'll get the tickets," I said. "It will be my treat!"
"In that case, okay," muttered Fly.

I went down to the circus grounds to work for
my tickets.
"Hmm," said the Boss. "I can use a good, strong spider."

He put me right to work.
I mended the nets and carried water to the fleas.

I painted wagon wheels

and washed dishes.

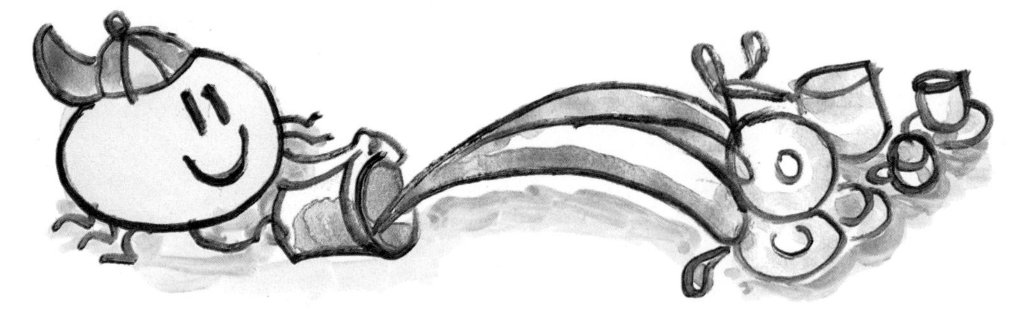

I pounded in stakes to hold up the tent.
It was hard work, but I needed those tickets.

I watched the fleas rehearse.
Trapeze artists flew through the air.
Clowns with painted faces and funny noses flipped and tumbled.

Jugglers juggled.
The fleas made the dog do dumb tricks.

The fleas made their home in the dog's shaggy coat. "There's no place like home," said a flea, bravely sticking his head inside the dog's mouth.

Finally everything was ready for the show.
"You did a good job, Spider," said the Boss of the flea circus. "Here's your free ticket."

"But I need three tickets," I said.
"Too bad," said the Boss.
"You can only have one."

I went over to Ladybug's house with the ticket.
"Here," I said, handing it to her. "You go."
"It won't be any fun to go alone," said Ladybug.
"I'll go," said Fly.

Then I got an idea.
"Hop onto my shoulders, Fly," I said. "Now you hop onto Fly's shoulders, Ladybug."

Then Ladybug brought out her aunt Ida's big coat, and we all got inside it. "On to the circus!" I said.

All the bugs in town were going.
The ticket taker gave us a funny look, but we all got in on one ticket.

The coat was very hot, and we were all glad to take
it off and sit down.
We waited and waited, but the show didn't start.

The bugs were getting impatient.
They began to stamp their feet and flap their wings.
"On with the show!" they hooted. "Let's get going, you fleas!"

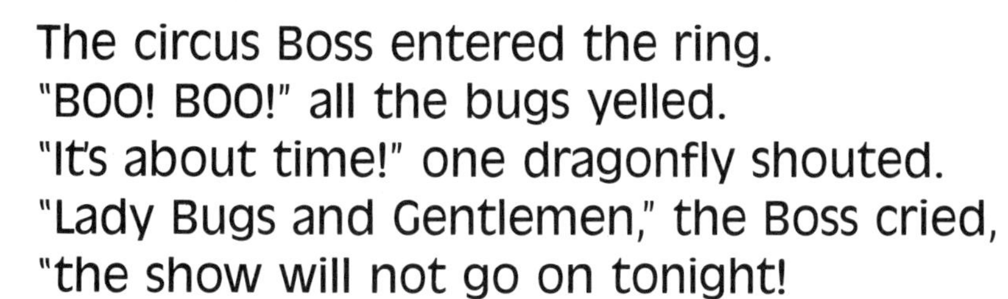
The circus Boss entered the ring.
"BOO! BOO!" all the bugs yelled.
"It's about time!" one dragonfly shouted.
"Lady Bugs and Gentlemen," the Boss cried,
"the show will not go on tonight!
The dog has run off with the performers!"

The bugs groaned and started throwing popcorn and peanuts.
They were angry—especially the bees.
"This looks like a sting," they droned.
"Somebody could get hurt," said Ladybug.

Then I got an idea!
I had watched the fleas rehearse.
I knew all the acts!

"Come on, Fly and Ladybug!" I said. "We're going to put on a show!"
"Goody," said Ladybug.
"Well, I don't know," grumbled Fly.

But put on a show we did.
And *what* a show!
We were clowns!

We were jugglers!

We were trapeze artists!
Miss Quito even joined us
on the high wire!

We had a really special *grande finale*.

The bugs really enjoyed the show, and only a few of them demanded their money back.

"You saved the circus," said the circus Boss.
"Thank you," I replied. "But I never could have done it without my friends."

The End.